TARZAN of the APES

adapted for young readers by
Robin Moore

from Edgar Rice Burroughs's
TARZAN OF THE APES

Illustrations by Jim Madsen

Aladdin Paperbacks

First Aladdin Paperbacks edition June 1999

Adaptation copyright © 1999 by Robin Moore. Adapted from *Tarzan of the Apes* by Edgar Rice Burroughs, originally published in the United States of America by A. C. McClurg & Co., 1914.

The trademark TARZAN® is owned by Edgar Rice Burroughs, Inc. This book has not been prepared, approved, licensed, or authorized by Edgar Rice Burroughs, Inc. or any other entity associated with the Edgar Rice Burroughs estate.

Interior illustrations copyright © 1999 by Simon & Schuster

Aladdin Paperbacks
An imprint of Simon & Schuster Children's Publishing Division
1230 Avenue of the Americas
New York, NY 10020

All rights reserved, including the right of reproduction
in whole or in part in any form.
Designed by Steve Scott
The text for this book is set in Bookman.
The illustrations in this book were rendered in pencil.
Printed and bound in the United States of America
10   9   8   7   6   5   4   3   2   1

Library of Congress Cataloging-in-Publication Data
Moore, Robin.
Tarzan of the apes / adaptation by Robin Moore.
— 1st Aladdin Paperbacks ed.   p.   cm.
Adapted from Tarzan of the apes by Edgar Rice Burroughs.
Summary: A baby boy, left alone in the African jungle after the deaths
of his parents, is adopted by an ape and raised to manhood without
ever seeing another human being.
ISBN 0-689-82413-0 (pbk.)
[1. Feral children—Fiction. 2. Apes—Fiction. 3. Jungles—Fiction.
4. Africa—Fiction.]
I. Burroughs, Edgar Rice, 1875-1950. Tarzan of the apes. II. Title.
PZ7.M78766Tar   1999
[Fic]—dc21   98-52894   CIP   AC

Introduction

Although the story you are about to read was first written more than eighty years ago, it is still as fresh and exciting as it was then, when Edgar Rice Burroughs imagined what it would be like to grow up in the wilds of the African jungle, surrounded by apes.

Over the years, Burroughs wrote twenty-six books about Tarzan of the Apes. Movies and comic books, radio and television programs, and the restless imaginations of generations of children have added to the story of Tarzan.

In this abridged retelling of *Tarzan of the Apes*, adapted especially for young readers, I have done my best to remain true to the spirit of the story as it appears in the original book, when Tarzan's tree-swinging adventures first sprang from Burroughs's fertile imagination.

—Robin Moore

Chapter One

On the west coast of Africa, not far from the place where the beautiful Congo River empties into the sea, a band of sixty apes roamed the dark forests and sunny grasslands. They were led by the great ape, Kerchak.

This was more than a hundred years ago, when very few people lived in jungles of the Congo. The land still belonged to the animals and the plant life and the singing insects.

Among the apes was one human—a small boy named Tarzan. In the language of the apes, Tarzan means "white ape."

Tarzan did not realize that he was a human being. He did not remember his true mother or father. The only parent he had ever known was Kala, the kind female ape, who had taken him from his cradle when he was one year old and

1

carried him off into the jungle to raise as her own son.

He could not speak. He ate and slept and acted like an animal. He had never seen a sailing ship or a pair of shoes or a map of England. For the longest time, he thought he was an animal, no different from his hairy cousins.

Then, one day, when the boy was ten years old, something happened that changed all that.

Kerchak's wanderings had taken the band of apes to a high mountain valley, where a deep lake lay like a mirror beneath the brilliant blue of the African sky.

Tarzan and his young cousin, Tulpak, were crouching by the water to drink. As he was about to dip his hands into the lake, the boy caught a glimpse of his reflection in the water.

His heart sank. He had never really looked at himself before.

When he compared himself to Tulpak, he was so ugly!

His little body, burned brown by the sun, was naked and shiny.

How he wished he could have a fine, silky coat, like Tulpak's.

His mouth was so small. He wanted a wide, grinning one, like Tulpak's. He was suddenly ashamed of his teeth. They were like little nubs compared to the fine yellow fangs of his cousin. And his nose: so small and pinched, not broad and majestic, with fine flaring nostrils.

The boy dipped his fingers into the lake and mixed up the water, as if he could make the memory of the image go away. But it was too late. He had seen. And for the first time, he realized that he was different from the others.

Tarzan wanted to forget. He cupped the water in his hands, closed his eyes, and drank.

4

He did not notice what was going on behind him. He did not hear the rustling in the tall grass. He didn't see the long, sleek body of the lioness, belly low to the ground, parting the dry stalks of grass as she crept up to the edge of the lakeshore. Sabor, the lioness, was hunting. Her eyes burned like green fire as she moved closer and closer to the small, huddled shapes.

Silently, she placed a huge blond paw on the pebbled shore. She was out of the grass now, within springing distance. Carefully, she drew her hind feet beneath her and poised, her muscles rippling with excitement. For a few moments, she crouched and waited, her eyes fixed on the naked backs of her prey.

Then, with a terrifying scream, she sprang.

Tarzan threw a look back over his

shoulder. Sabor's open mouth was a blur of white and red and yellow.

Tulpak squealed and rolled to the side. Like all apes, he feared the water and scrambled for the safety of the trees. But Tarzan obeyed his own instincts. Tarzan sprang forward, into the deep water.

Suddenly, he was surrounded by the cold blue of the lake. Tarzan sank to the bottom. He could not help it. He had never learned to swim and he was afraid of the water. But right now he was even more afraid of Sabor.

At any moment, he expected to feel the sharp claws of the lion sinking into his back or the powerful jaws closing around his tender shoulder. But there was nothing—only the cool embrace of the water and the popping of bubbles around his face.

Furiously, he paddled with his hands and kicked with his feet, heading for the surface. Even though he had never dared to enter the water before, young Tarzan was swimming, swimming for his life.

Chapter Two

As he swam, horrible pictures of Sabor's teeth and claws flooded Tarzan's mind. His fear made his arms and legs move faster.

When Tarzan reached the center of the lake, he looked back over his shoulder.

There was Sabor, pacing back and forth on the shore, lashing her tail in anger. She had not tried to follow him. The big cat was no swimmer.

As Tulpac laughed from the tree above her, Sabor knew she was defeated. With a nasty snarl, the lioness dipped her large head and slinked away into the tall grass.

The boy swam for shore with smooth, graceful strokes.

When he reached the bank, Tulpac and a dozen other apes were there to greet him. They wiped the water from his smooth skin with their rough, hairy hands. This was how Tarzan learned to love the water. Although the apes refused to follow him, they watched curiously each day as the boy dove and swam in the cool blue lake.

One day, Tarzan decided to explore the river. Now that he knew how to swim, his fear of the water was replaced with curiosity. The boy set off downstream, following the twists and turns of the Congo as it made its way to the sea.

Within an hour, he stood on the beach. Tarzan gasped when he saw the wide blue ocean. This was nothing like the treetop world of his ape family. This was something entirely new.

As Tarzan wandered along the beach, he noticed what looked like a massive rock tucked back in a grove of banana trees. But when he came closer, he could see that it was made of many pieces of wood.

Without realizing what he was seeing, the boy circled the walls of the cabin again and again, running his hands over the rough logs. He found the windows and peered through the wooden bars, sniffing the air.

At last, by accident, he pushed open the door.

It creaked loudly as it swung back, showing him a world beyond anything he could have imagined. The walls were covered with shelves of books. The floor was carpeted with soft animal skins.

The tables and chairs were arranged neatly, with cups and bowls and cooking pots sitting exactly as their owners had left them. A breeze drifted through the open window, rocking a wooden cradle that sat by the bed.

Tarzan stepped into the room.

That was when he noticed the

skeletons. One lay on the bed. The other was sprawled on the floor, not far from the door. The bones and skulls were bleached white.

They did not interest Tarzan. He had seen many dead animals in the jungle and he did not give them more than a passing glance. Instead, his eyes were filled with the wonder of the man-made things that surrounded him.

Tarzan had no way of knowing that these brittle bones were all that remained of his mother and father. He did not know that the cabin he had entered was built by his father, and that the cradle that lay at his feet had once belonged to him.

Ten years before, Tarzan's parents had come to Africa to make a new life. His father and mother, John and Alice Clayton, were known as Lord and Lady Greystoke. They were wealthy and respected people in London, England.

They lived in a castle that their family had owned for generations.

The Greystokes had traveled to Africa to do important work for their government. They had been asked to live among the African people and learn all they could about this beautiful continent, a land that Europeans had just begun to explore. Lord and Lady Greystoke had planned to build a home and raise a family in Africa.

But their plans fell apart, even before they arrived. The crew of their sailing ship rebelled against their cruel captain and, one night, they killed him. They took over the ship and left Lord and Lady Greystoke to survive on the wild coast of Africa.

With only a few simple tools, the Greystokes made a life there in the wilderness. Lord Greystoke built a cabin on the beach, and Lady Alice learned to make meals from the wild fruits of the jungle. During this time, she gave birth to a healthy boy, whom they named Johnny, after his father.

At night, by the light of a candle, the young mother read to her Johnny and rocked him to sleep in a cradle Lord Greystoke had made from a hollowed-out tree trunk. These were happy times. But they did not last.

When the boy was a year old, Lady Alice died of a fever. Lord Greystoke couldn't do anything to save her. And he was worried about how he would care for his son. The infant thrashed in his cradle, day and night, crying for his mother's milk.

One day, while Lord Greystoke was sitting on his doorstep, the great ape, Kerchak, crept from the jungle. His band was roaming near the beach, and he smelled the smoke from the cabin chimney.

The ape, who had always been known

for his terrible temper, was enraged to find someone in his territory. The huge beast rushed at the man. The Englishman rose to his feet. But he had no weapon and he was no match for the awesome strength of the bull ape. Kerchak smashed Lord Greystoke's skull and wandered off, leaving his body in the doorway.

The baby began to cry. His wails drifted out the open door of the cabin, into the jungle. That was when the kind female ape Kala heard him. One of her own babies had died a few days before. When she heard the boy's hungry cries, her heart went out to him. Cautiously, the female crept toward the sound.

In the shadows of the tiny room, Kala lifted the thrashing boy from his cradle and held him to her chest, offering him her sweet milk. He looked up into her face and smiled.

From that moment forward, he was

no longer a young English lord. Instead, he became a wild thing, Tarzan of the apes.

And now, many years later, Tarzan had found his way back to the place where he had been born.

Everywhere he looked, he saw fascinating things. His father's hunting knife lay on the table by the window.

Attracted by the shining blade, the boy reached out to pick it up. But the sharp edge sliced into his fingers. Tarzan drew back, looking down at the knife. At last, he cautiously picked it up by the handle. In a short time, he was sitting on the floor, using the blade to carve marks in the wooden boards. His eyes shone with delight.

Tarzan turned to the shelves and ran his hands over the books. They tumbled to the floor, with their pages falling open. Tarzan crouched over the books and cocked his head, staring at the pages.

The one that attracted him the most was a child's alphabet book, which his mother had brought to teach her children to read. It contained letters and colorful pictures.

Tarzan stared for a long time at the page.

And this is what it said:

A IS FOR APE.

B IS FOR BOY.

Tarzan did not remember that his mother had shown him this page many times.

But he did know that the pictures of the apes reminded him of Tulpak and Kerchak and Kala. The picture of the boy looked a lot like him.

Outside, the darkness was closing in on the jungle and the cabin. Tarzan knew that he must return to his ape

17

family in the trees. He decided that he would take the knife with him.

As he rose to leave, he noticed one more thing that delighted his eye. It was a necklace—a locket with a golden chain and a sparkling diamond, which lay around the neck of Lady Alice's skeleton. Carefully, Tarzan lifted the necklace from his mother's neck and placed it around his own.

Then, closing the door softly behind him, the boy slipped into the jungle.

Chapter Three

As he grew to manhood, Tarzan returned to the cabin again and again, learning a little more each time. He spent hours puzzling over the man-made objects that lay inside the cabin walls. But nothing fascinated him more than the books, with their colorful pictures and strange markings.

At first, Tarzan thought the black letters were bugs with tiny, twisting legs. But when he tried to pluck them from the page, his fingers came away empty.

But his mind was not empty. Tarzan spent hours leafing through the books, comparing the pictures of the objects and the bug-marks.

Slowly, the bugs became his friends. He saw them appear again and again, until he knew their twisting shapes, just as he would know the shape of an animal's track on the jungle floor.

No ape could have taught himself to read and write from those books. But Tarzan was not an ape; he was an intelligent, curious boy.

By the time he was eighteen years old, Tarzan could read most of the books in his father's collection. Tarzan also discovered pencil and paper and taught himself to write, copying the bug-marks in the books. But he could not speak. The only language Tarzan knew was the language of the apes.

Tarzan's body had been growing along with his mind. The challenges of jungle life had hardened his muscles and sharpened his senses. He could run and swim and swing through the trees as well as any jungle creature.

Now, when Tarzan looked into the water of the lake, here is what he saw:

His face was handsome and intelligent. His hair was black and glossy and fell long on his naked shoulders. Around his neck, he wore his mother's necklace. His only clothing was a square of deerskin, which he wrapped around his waist. On his belt hung his father's knife, in a dark leather sheath. He used the razor-sharp blade to scrape the sprouting hairs from his chin and cheeks, so that he would look more like the men he saw in his picture books.

Tarzan lived with his ape family. But he knew he was different and he felt out-of-place. Kerchak had always treated Tarzan as an outsider.

And now that the white ape was becoming tall and strong-armed, the leader saw him as a threat. Kerchak would sometimes snarl and chase Tarzan off from the rest of the band, glaring at him with reddened eyes.

The young man resisted the temptation

to fight back, knowing that it was forbidden. Kerchak saw this as a sign of weakness and never lost an opportunity to bully Tarzan, shaming him before the rest of the band. It was only Kala's kindness that made life among the apes bearable. Sometimes, when he was feeling very bad, Tarzan wondered what it would be like to see one of his own kind.

Then, one day, Tarzan got his wish.

It was early morning. One by one, the apes were swinging down from the trees, leaving the safety of their sleeping places to begin another day of wandering on the jungle floor. Kala and Tarzan were moving slowly along an old elephant trail, turning over rotten logs to search for sweet-tasting bugs.

Kala was old and gray. Her teeth were worn down to almost nothing, and it was not easy for her to find soft food to eat. Sometimes, Tarzan climbed high and gathered fruit, which he fed her with his fingers, just as she had done to him when he was a naked, helpless baby.

Suddenly, Kala made a strange coughing sound and dropped to the ground. Instantly, Tarzan was at her side. When he bent over her, he saw that a shaft of wood, with bird feathers tied to the end, was driven deep into her chest.

Tarzan tried to pull the stick free. But it would not come loose. Kala's lips moved. But no sound came out.

Then Tarzan heard a whizzing sound. He lifted his head in time to see another one of the bird-sticks come flying through the air and stick in the ground beside him.

Peering back into the trees, Tarzan saw a man holding a long stick, bent with a string.

The instant their eyes met, the archer turned and fled down the trail.

Chapter Four

Tarzan held Kala in his arms as the clearing filled with apes. They chattered and squealed and crowded around the wounded female. Tarzan watched in helpless disbelief as the light faded from Kala's kind old eyes and her mouth stopped moving. Her lifeless body sagged in his arms.

Tarzan was filled with rage—and sadness. Kala was the only mother he had ever known. Now Tarzan stood, towering above the chattering heads of the apes. He peered back into the jungle. Where was the man?

In a flash, Tarzan took to the trees, swinging through the branches at lightning speed, ruled by the law of the jungle. The ape man would find Kala's murderer and kill him.

After he had traveled for several

furious moments, Tarzan stopped, balancing on a swaying branch. He caught a glimpse of movement on the elephant trail beneath his feet.

Forty feet below, Tarzan could see the running figure of a young African tribesman. For a moment, Tarzan could not move. Despite his anger, he was amazed to see a man, like himself. But his surprise could not cool the savage anger that pumped through his veins. The ape man gripped a vine and swung down.

When Tarzan reached the spot above the man's head, he drew his knife and dropped through the trees. Tarzan landed on his enemy's back, knocking him to the ground. In a moment, Tarzan drove his knife into the man, who died, just as Kala had, without speaking a word.

Tarzan stood over his enemy, breathing heavily. He looked at the man's hands and chest and face.

Yes, Tarzan thought, this is no ape. This is a man, like myself.

Tarzan had often killed, for food and to protect his family. He was proud when his enemies fell before him. But this time, he felt different. He did not feel any joy or pride, only a strange sadness.

Tarzan turned his attention to the hunter's bow and his quiver of arrows. He decided to take them with him. Slinging the bow and quiver across his back, Tarzan leaped up, caught a branch, and climbed high into the trees.

When he reached a place that was more than two hundred feet from the ground, he smelled the smoke of cooking fires and heard the musical sound of human voices. Guided by his senses, he swung along through the trees.

He was soon peering down on a clearing in the forest. There, along a jungle stream, he saw a circle of huts with roofs made from river grass. To

his astonishment, he saw dozens of humans—old and young, male and female—moving about in the clearing.

The ape man spent the rest of the day crouched on the branch, watching the villagers. A part of him wanted to be among them, listening to the music they made with their mouths and looking into their bright eyes.

But he knew he could not: He had killed one of their sons. And he knew that one of their sons had killed Kala.

Tarzan felt empty and cold. Now that Kala was gone, he would not return to the apes. He was not a white ape. He was a man.

But the men in the village below were now his enemies. Tarzan peered back into the jungle. His eyes were blurring with tears of rage and grief.

In all of his life, he had never felt so alone.

Chapter Five

Tarzan returned to the cabin and spent many days sitting in his father's chair, reading Lord Greystoke's books. He also practiced with the bow and arrows. Within a month, he was an expert shot.

One day, while he was hunting in the trees along the beach, he saw a white square floating in the ocean waves, far out to sea. As the wind blew it closer, Tarzan could see that it was a huge sailing ship. He had seen pictures of these boats in his father's books.

As the ship pulled close to shore, he saw men on her decks.

Tarzan's heart soared at the thought of meeting other people. Not all people were cruel. He knew that from reading his books. But he wondered: Would these visitors be friends or enemies?

He would hide in the trees and find out. Before he left the cabin, Tarzan spread a white piece of paper on the table. He took a lead pencil and carefully wrote:

This is the house of Tarzan.
Do not harm the things
that are Tarzan's.
Tarzan watches.
TARZAN OF THE APES

He stuck the notice onto the door and closed it tightly. Then he slipped into the trees and climbed to a place where he could see without being seen.

The ship sailed into the lagoon and dropped anchor, lowering a rowboat. Several people climbed into the boat and began pulling for shore. When they waded through the surf, Tarzan counted twenty people on his beach.

They were not like the villagers. They were pale-skinned, like himself. They were dressed in many layers of clothing, and most of them carried long, shining poles that Tarzan knew from his reading were guns.

Fifteen were members of the crew—middle-aged men, dressed roughly and carrying weapons. But the remaining five were different. They were three men and two women.

Tarzan studied them closely. Two of the men were white-haired and wearing spectacles. One of them walked with a cane. The younger man was about Tarzan's age and was handsomely dressed in black boots, a safari jacket, and a pith helmet.

Of the women, one was heavy and had a loud voice and colorful clothing. But it was the young female who interested Tarzan the most.

She was the loveliest thing he had ever seen. A cloud of blond hair fell long on her shoulders. Her feet and hands

33

were small, like a child's. Her eyes were soft and kind, like Kala's.

When the men with guns spotted the cabin, they gave a shout and herded the smaller group toward it, pushing them roughly along. One of the men poked the girl with the barrel of his gun. Tarzan could hardly control himself. Tarzan wanted to break his skull.

But he made himself stay in the trees. He did not understand what was happening. The rough men pushed the five unarmed people into the cabin and closed the door behind them. Then the men dashed for the boat, hopped aboard, and pushed off into the surf.

Tarzan watched as they rowed to the ship and climbed aboard. They set their sails and began to move up the coast. The ape man watched the door of the cabin. The people were not coming out. But he wanted to make sure the evil men were not coming back. He swung into the trees and climbed very high, keeping the ship in sight.

The crew did not go more than a few miles before they dropped anchor and rowed their boat ashore.

The ape man reached the line of trees just as the crew waded onto the beach. They took a huge wooden box from the boat and carried it up onto the sand.

On a little hill overlooking the beach, they dug a deep hole and buried the box. Then the men counted their steps and wrote everything down on a piece of paper.

In an hour they were rowing back to their boat. They sailed far out to sea, leaving Tarzan to puzzle over what he had seen.

Tarzan didn't like these men. If they wanted to get rid of the box, they could have simply thrown it overboard. But they were hiding it. Maybe they would come back for it later. Tarzan decided to keep their box.

He went to the spot, dug up the huge chest, and dragged it across the sand. He hid the box in a huge, hollow tree. The box was closed with metal, and even Tarzan's strength was not enough to open it. Tarzan did not spend more time on the box. For now, he wanted to go back to the cabin, to see how the visitors were enjoying the house of Tarzan.

Chapter Six

When Tarzan got back to the beach, he saw that the cabin door was closed and smoke was coming from the chimney. His visitors were making themselves at home. He wondered what he should do.

He saw that his note had been taken from the door. This meant that they had read his words. Now, the ape man thought, I will go to them. But before he could rise from his hiding place, he saw the door open.

The young man in the strange hat was there. He was looking off into the jungle. He closed the door firmly and walked into the trees. Tarzan watched. What was he after? Firewood? Water? Was he hunting or gathering food?

Tarzan followed him into the jungle.

A short while later, the ape man could tell that the young explorer was lost. Even though the young man was within shouting distance of the cabin, he wandered aimlessly through the thick jungle. Tarzan crouched on a tree branch overhead.

It was then that the ape man saw Numa the lion approaching with quiet, careful steps. Numa was hungry.

Tarzan fitted an arrow to his bowstring and aimed at the lion's ribs. A moment later, the shaft was singing through the air, burying its sharp point in the lion's side.

Numa roared, and snapped at the arrow with his massive jaws. Tarzan dropped from the trees and landed on the beast's broad back. With one arm, he held the lion's throat; with the other, he drew his knife and plunged the long blade into the lion's heart.

The beast dropped forward and lay on the ground like a mountain of blond fur.

The young man watched as Tarzan

39

wiped the lion's blood from his knife and placed it in his sheath.

"Thank you," he said at last, "whoever you are. I can't thank you enough."

But Tarzan was not listening. He threw the young man onto his back and began climbing a mass of twisted vines. Soon they were high above the jungle floor.

The young explorer rode like a child on the ape man's muscular back as he leaped from one branch to another. He did not look down. The man knew that if they fell, they would both be killed instantly.

When they reached the edge of the trees, Tarzan dropped the young man to the ground, then disappeared back into the jungle.

On shaking legs, the explorer walked to the cabin and went inside.

~~~

Tarzan waited until dark, then crept

to the window of the cabin. He watched and listened, but did not understand what was happening. The visitors divided the room in half by hanging a blanket across a long rope. The men slept on one side, the women on the other.

Soon the room was filled with the snores of the exhausted travelers. But Tarzan saw that the young woman could not sleep. He watched as she lit a candle and seated herself at the table by the window.

She took paper and pen from her bag and began to write. He noticed that her eyes were moist with tears and that she stopped several times to read the words to herself before continuing. After she had filled both sides of a sheet of paper, she sighed and folded the letter, leaving it on the table.

When the young girl blew out the candle and went to bed, she had no idea that she was being watched. Tarzan sat in the darkness outside the window, gazing on her beauty with wide, curious eyes.

He wanted to see what she had written. Tarzan reached in through the bars of the open window and silently closed his hand around the letter. He tucked it into his belt. A moment later, he was high overhead, among the swaying branches.

In the morning, when the light was strong, he would read what the light-haired girl had to say.

Chapter Seven

Tarzan bent over the piece of paper in the early morning sunlight. The bugs would speak to him now, telling him what was in the girl's mind. As he read, the ape man felt his heart opening.

This is what he read:

To: Hazel Strong
Baltimore, Maryland
Date: February 3, 1909
Location: Somewhere on the west coast
*   of Africa*

Dear Hazel,
*   It's silly for me to write this letter, because I don't know if I will ever get a chance to mail it. But I simply must tell someone about all of the strange and terrible things that have happened on this trip to Africa.*
*   As you know, I did not want to come.*

But Father and Mr. Philander would not give me a moment's peace until I promised to join them. It's a good thing I did, too. They may be brilliant college professors, but neither of them has any common sense whatsoever. I am glad I brought our housekeeper, Esmeralda, and our good friend William Clayton along. They have been very helpful.

Hazel, do you remember William? You met him at the house once. His uncle and aunt were Lord and Lady Greystoke, the famous English couple who were lost at sea while coming to Africa years ago.

Because they never had any children, all of the family fortune has passed to William. In England, since his uncle's death, William has been called Lord Greystoke. I think he wants to marry me. I am not sure I want to marry him. But Father wants me to marry an American—that dreadful man, Mr. Canler. I am so confused. I don't want to disappoint Father, but I want to be happy.

You will remember that old treasure

map Father found at the rare book shop. He was determined to follow it. I found out later that he had borrowed $10,000 from Mr. Canler to afford this expedition. I was sure that Father had made another one of his foolish investments.

But I was wrong. We found the treasure. A chest containing a fortune in gold coins! It was right where the map said it would be, buried on an island off the west coast of Africa.

We thought all was well and headed home. But then our troubles really began. The crew of our ship decided they wanted the treasure for themselves. They killed their captain and took charge of the ship. They were going to kill us, too. But William convinced them to put us ashore here on the coast.

We are staying at the cabin of a man named Tarzan. He must be an Englishman. He wrote us a most unusual letter and posted it on the door. But we haven't met him yet.

Tonight, William got lost in the jungle

and said he was saved by a savage man who swings through the trees like an ape. I hope he is not a cannibal. Maybe when Mr. Tarzan returns, he will tell us who this man might be.

Hazel, I am frightened. We have only a little food and a few supplies. It may be a very long time before we are rescued. I am not certain that I will ever see the civilized world again.

I am very tired. I must try to sleep now.

Your friend,
Jane Porter

When he finished reading, Tarzan folded the letter and stuck it into his belt. He was confused. He did not understand everything in the letter. But one thing was clear: She needed help.

So, she wanted food, did she? Tarzan would provide. He waded into the river and quickly caught a dozen fish. Slipping up to the cabin while everyone was still asleep, he left his catch hanging by a string from a tree branch, where the visitors would be sure to see it.

Each day, Tarzan brought fresh meat and fruit to the cabin. A few times, the girl called out to him. But he would not stay. He was too shy. He preferred to watch her from a distance. He noticed that sometimes she watched him, too. Her eyes were wide and curious.

At last, Tarzan got the idea of writing her a letter. He wanted to tell the girl his feelings. He spent a long time figuring out what to say. When he slipped the folded sheet of paper into the window one night, this is what it said:

I am Tarzan of the Apes. I want you to live here in my house forever. I will hunt for you and keep you safe. You are Jane Porter. I saw your name in the letter I took. I have read your words. I know your heart.

Now you know mine. I love you.
Will you love me?

TARZAN OF THE APES

When Jane read the words the next day, she was struck by their honesty and power. Who was this strange Englishman? Why didn't he come forward and introduce himself? And how could he love her when they had never even met?

Lost in thought over the contents of the letter, Jane wandered among the trees at the edge of the jungle. One step led to another. At last, she was standing in a silent grove of majestic trees. At her feet was a clump of graceful flowers.

She bent and was about to pluck an orchid from its stem when, suddenly, a huge, hairy arm encircled her waist.

The next thing she knew, she was being carried up into the trees, far from the safety of the ground. She tried to twist around to see the face of her attacker. But she could not. She tried to break free, but the huge arm held her firmly. All she could do was open her mouth and scream.

Chapter Eight

Terkoz was a huge ape who had once been a member of Kerchak's band. But he had been cast out for being mean-tempered and cruel to the females. When the huge ape saw the young woman wandering in the quiet of the forest, he decided to carry her away.

Tarzan was dozing on a branch in the treetops when he heard Jane's scream. He jumped up and caught a vine, swinging through the trees. Within moments, he was looking down on Terkoz. The ape had carried the girl to the base of a large tree. When Terkoz looked up with bloodshot eyes, he saw Tarzan sliding down the trunk.

Terkoz cast the girl aside and roared a challenge to the ape man. They came together like charging bulls. Jane watched in horror as the two jungle

fighters snarled and wrestled on the ground. Terkoz's teeth closed around the ape man's bulging arm muscles.

But Tarzan was fast. He drew his knife and thrust it into the ape's hairy chest, again and again. Even with such terrible wounds, the big ape continued to fight. But he could not fight for long. Like a huge tree falling from a great height, the ape fell backward and landed in the grass, turning the green leaves red with his blood.

Tarzan picked Jane Porter up in his arms. She was so small and light, almost like a child. He could carry her easily through the treetops.

Tarzan's first thought was to return her to the cabin. But then he would be without her. He couldn't bear that thought. Instead, he clutched her to his chest and leaped up into the trees, scrambling from one branch to the next until they were far, far above the jungle floor. They were in his world.

When Jane glanced down, she felt light-headed. But when she looked into Tarzan's eyes, her fear left her. She had never met anyone like this. This forest man was strong and agile, like a Greek god in one of her father's mythology books. But he was also shy, like a young boy on his first date.

And Tarzan had never seen anything like Jane. He could not stop looking at her lovely face and her shining eyes. For the two of them, the rest of the world disappeared, and all that mattered was their joy in looking at each other.

"I don't know who you are," Jane said, "but I owe you my life. What you did was so brave. . . ."

Jane stopped. Tarzan was frowning. She could tell that he did not understand her words. It was then that Jane saw the locket around his neck. "How strange," she said, pointing to the necklace.

Tarzan took the gleaming jewel from around his neck and placed it in her palm.

Her fingers fumbled with the locket until she opened it, gazing at two small oval photographs—the images of Tarzan's parents, Lord and Lady Greystoke.

Jane was thunderstruck. She glanced from the photo of the Englishman in proper evening dress to the face of the wild man who sat beside her. The similarity was striking. But, how? And why?

There were too many unanswered questions. Jane looked up at Tarzan. He was a savage, she knew that. But she was not afraid of him. His face held a tenderness that was almost heartbreaking.

She found herself imagining him beside her at an elegant dinner party back in Baltimore. He was speaking perfect English and was dressed like the handsome man in the locket.

But then she realized that this was a foolish thought. He was a forest man, fed on red meat and wild fruits. He was wild. But he was also good and kind and very, very, brave.

Jane Porter glanced around her, taking in the beauty of his wild world: The sun was streaming down through the holes in the treetops now, sending arrows of light through the misty morning air. The jungle smelled green and alive.

Chapter Nine

Professor Porter and his band of treasure hunters had visitors. A ship appeared on the shore. William Clayton lit signal fires on the beach, and everyone shouted until the ship turned into the wind and dropped its anchor in the lagoon.

In a short time, a boat was lowered, and men in white uniforms came wading ashore.

One dashing young officer with a long mustache extended his hand to William. "I am Lieutenant D'Arnot, of the French navy," he said in excellent English. "We ran down a band of cutthroats sailing along the coast. When we questioned them, they confessed that they had left you here to die. We are here to rescue you. I am glad we arrived in time."

"Thank you," William said, "but one of our party is still missing—a young woman who wandered off into the jungle."

"She is my daughter," the professor said, "and I am afraid I will never see her again."

The officer frowned. "How long has she been gone?" he asked.

Professor Porter sighed. "Since this morning. We have been searching for her all day."

D'Arnot placed a hand on the older man's shoulder. "Don't worry," he said, "I will send some men to find her. In fact, I will lead the search party myself."

In an hour, the brave lieutenant and a troop of thirty men began to comb the jungle for Jane Porter. They headed east, following an old elephant trail.

Shortly after the search party left, Tarzan brought Jane safely to the cabin. He dropped her on the edge of the clearing, and they stood together for a moment.

Neither of them wanted to say good-bye.

Jane reached out and took Tarzan's large hand in hers. She placed the locket into his outstretched palm and gently closed his fingers around it.

Something told her she could not accept this gift. She knew that it was very precious, too closely tied to the forest man's past. Jane felt confused. She felt both grateful and sad. She wished that she could speak to him, telling him how much she admired his generosity and his kindness. . . .

Just then, they heard the sound of gunfire back in the jungle.

Before Jane could say anything, Tarzan turned and swung up into the trees. The ape man did not know about the search party or the boat. All he knew was that gunfire meant death.

And if he could do anything to prevent the death of these brave people, he would.

As he swung along, the sound of the Frenchmen's rifles carried far in the green world.

It did not take Tarzan long to find the spot where the Africans had ambushed the Frenchmen. The fight had been sudden and bloody.

All the Africans had known was that strange men with strange weapons were moving into their territory, toward their village. The Africans had fought to protect themselves and their families.

D'Arnot and his men had not seen the warriors crouching with their bows along the trail. Suddenly, the air had been filled with the sound of flying arrows and the cries of dying men. The French had taken their wounded and pulled back into the jungle. But D'Arnot had refused to retreat until the last of his men were carried to safety. Soon his ammunition was gone, and the warriors had rushed around him, taking him prisoner.

Now Tarzan peered down into the village and saw the brave officer tied to a post. He was covered with wounds. But he moved his head, and Tarzan knew that he was still alive.

When darkness fell, the ape man dropped to the ground and slipped into the circle of huts. His knife sliced through the prisoner's ropes. Before anyone in the village knew what was happening, Tarzan had carried the Frenchman up into the safety of the trees.

Tarzan put many miles between himself and the African warriors. He found a hiding place in the jungle where D'Arnot could rest and heal from his wounds.

The ape man wanted to return to the cabin, to let the others know that the man was safe. But he was afraid to

61

leave him alone. He was afraid he might die if Tarzan was not there to watch over him. Tarzan would wait.

Slowly, D'Arnot opened his eyes. He thought he was dreaming when he saw that he was no longer in the village but high in the trees, far above the ground. When he saw Tarzan sitting on a limb beside him, he spoke to him in French.

But Tarzan only shook his head. D'Arnot tried English, German, and a few of the African tribal languages. But Tarzan only looked at him blankly.

Then the ape man took a smooth piece of bark and pulled a lead pencil from his quiver. D'Arnot was astonished. But he was even more surprised when the savage man wrote:

I am Tarzan of the Apes. Who are you? Can you read this language?

The officer looked at the bark and

nodded weakly. "I speak English," he said, "I am—"

But Tarzan simply shook his head, handing the man the pencil.

D'Arnot thought that maybe Tarzan was deaf and could only understand written words. The Frenchman wrote:

I am Paul D'Arnot, an officer in the French navy. I want to thank you for saving my life. May I ask why you can write English but cannot speak it?

Tarzan read the words and seized a new piece of bark, writing quickly.

I speak only the language of the jungle animals. I have lived in the jungle all my life. This is the first time I have been able to speak to another man through written words.

D'Arnot nodded and wrote:

Incredible! I am honored. But tell me this: I came to rescue a woman named Jane Porter. Have you seen her?

Tarzan nodded. He wrote:

I know Jane Porter. She is safe at the cabin by the beach.

D'Arnot nodded. He was too tired to write anymore. He closed his eyes and slept.

Suffering from a fever, he slept for five days. Tarzan washed his wounds and gave him water to drink. At last, the officer was well enough to stand and walk on his own, although he was still very unsteady.

D'Arnot wrote this message to Tarzan:

You have saved me. What can I do to thank you?

Tarzan grinned and wrote:

Teach me to speak the language of men.

The officer smiled. He replied:

I will teach you to speak in both French and English.

Tarzan frowned. He wrote:

I do not understand.

D'Arnot grinned.

How foolish of me. Let me explain. If all the apes of the world were in one place, they would speak one language. But it is not so with men. Men speak many different languages. In the entire world, there are hundreds of groups of men, each speaking in their own way. French and English are but two of these groups. But most educated people speak more than one language.

Tarzan nodded.

It was then that his lessons began. D'Arnot began by pointing out familiar objects and helping Tarzan to say both the French and English words for each thing. It was not long before they were speaking in simple sentences.

One day D'Arnot woke and stretched in the morning sunlight. "I am strong enough to travel," he said. "Take me to the cabin of Tarzan of the Apes."

The ape man smiled. "We will go now," he said.

Taking the Frenchman on his back, they traveled swiftly. Tarzan was eager to talk with Jane Porter, to hear her voice speaking to him again.

But when they arrived at the cabin, it was empty.

Chapter Ten

Jane had left a note on the cabin door.

To Tarzan of the Apes:

Thank you for letting us use your cabin. A French ship has come to take us away. We must go quickly because the men were attacked and many were killed—even their leader, a man named D'Arnot.

I am sorry I never met you. Thank you for your wonderful letter. I don't know how you came to love me. But I must be honest: My father has already chosen a husband for me back in America, and I cannot disappoint him. I am sorry.

Also, I want to thank the forest man who rescued me from the ape. If you see him, please tell him that I will always be grateful. If any of you are ever in Baltimore, Maryland, America, you will always be welcome in the Porter house.

JANE PORTER

Tarzan's eyes flew over the words. As he read, his heart sank.

D'Arnot simply shook his head and placed his hand on the ape man's shoulder. "I am sorry, my friend," he said quietly.

"I must go to America," Tarzan vowed. "She does not know that I am both Tarzan and the forest man!"

D'Arnot smiled sadly. "It is very far away," he explained. "You would have to travel on a boat for many days."

"I will go mad if I stay here without this Jane Porter," Tarzan replied.

D'Arnot looked into Tarzan's eyes and could see that he was serious. "In order to ride on the boat, you would need a lot of money," he said.

Tarzan wrinkled his brow. "Money?" he asked. "What is that?"

D'Arnot laughed. "It is a piece of paper to show how much you have earned. Of course, there are many things that are valuable and can be sold for money."

Tarzan thought of the box he had seen the men bury. He wondered if that could be valuable. When he told D'Arnot about the buried chest, the Frenchman became very interested.

He asked Tarzan to take him to the hollow tree where the box was hidden. He used a rock to break open the iron lock. When he swung back the lid, they were both astonished to see that the chest was filled to the brim with golden coins.

"Will this be enough?" Tarzan asked.

D'Arnot smiled. "More than enough, my friend. But we must remember that this treasure rightfully belongs to Professor Porter.

"Listen: I owe you my life. Back in Paris, I have more money than a man really needs. It would give me great pleasure to pay for your trip to America. For now, we must walk north and hire a ship to come back and pick up this treasure. Then we will go to France, and you will go to America."

Tarzan shook his head. "You cannot walk north now," he said.

"No, not now. But soon. Take me back to the cabin so we can rest."

Back at the cabin, D'Arnot admired the shelves of books. "Have you read all of these books?" he asked.

"All but a few. There is one with writing I could not understand," Tarzan said. He pulled the book with the strange bug-marks from the shelf and handed it to the officer.

D'Arnot ran his eyes over the first page of the book.

"Incredible!" he exclaimed. "This is Lord Greystoke's diary. It is written in French. He must have been an educated man."

All that afternoon, D'Arnot sat in a chair by the window and read to Tarzan.

It was all there: The terrors of the ocean voyage and the treachery of the angry sailors, the horror of being left alone on the African coast, the joy of little John Clayton's birth and the sorrow of Lady Alice's death.

One of the happier pages read:

"My boy is as alert and cheerful as a young monkey. And as full of mischief—here, as if to prove the truth of my words, he has spilled my ink bottle and placed his finger marks on the page!"

Along the edge of the page, D'Arnot saw four wee finger marks and a tiny thumbprint. "This would clear up the mystery once and for all," the Frenchman said. "I know a police detective in Paris who can compare your fingerprints with the ones on this page. If they match, that will prove it!"

Tarzan wrinkled his brow. "Prove what?" he asked.

D'Arnot laughed loudly. "Why, Tarzan, don't you see? You were the young babe! These are your fingerprints. Lord Greystoke and Lady Alice were your parents. You are Johnny Clayton, the heir to the Greystoke fortune!"

"No," Tarzan said. "Kala was my mother; my father was a white ape."

D'Arnot smiled patiently. "Come to Paris with me, my friend. I will prove that what I say is true."

Tarzan stared long and hard at the ink-spotted page. Silently, he placed his broad, strong hand over the tiny hand-print of the infant.

"Yes," the ape man whispered, "we will go."

Chapter Eleven

In Paris, D'Arnot took Tarzan to a bank, which gave him American money in exchange for the treasure. The police took Tarzan's fingerprints. Then they consulted a fingerprint expert.

"This case is very difficult," the man said. "I will need more time to determine if these prints were truly made by the same person, seventeen years apart. Leave both the diary and the recent fingerprints with me. I will send word as soon as I have made a determination."

Tarzan could not wait any longer. He said good-bye to D'Arnot and boarded a ship for America. He promised to send D'Arnot a telegram as soon as he located Jane Porter.

Tarzan no longer looked like a savage. D'Arnot had taught him how to dress and groom himself. He could eat and talk and shake hands like a gentleman.

~⌒~

Tarzan went to America by ship and arrived in the Baltimore harbor in early summer. He was able to find the house of Professor Porter. But when he arrived, he was told that Jane Porter and her father, as well as William Clayton and Robert Canler, had all gone to the family farm in Wisconsin.

Tarzan sent a telegram to D'Arnot and made the long train ride to Wisconsin. He had come halfway around the world, all for the chance to see Jane Porter's face and hear her musical voice.

When he knocked on the door of the farmhouse, Professor Porter himself answered.

Tarzan could tell by the look on his face that the old man did not recognize him.

"Where is Jane Porter?" he asked.

But before the professor could answer,

Jane walked into the room. She stared at the well-dressed man on her doorstep. Her hand went to her mouth. "No," she said, "it can't be—you are the forest man!"

"Yes," he said, "but I have learned to be civilized."

Jane stepped forward and touched the front of his fine coat. "You have changed so much," she said, leading him inside.

"Not really," Tarzan answered. "One thing about me that has not changed is my love for you. In your note you said that you could not love me. But maybe you did not know that I am Tarzan, the one who wrote you the love letter. I am also the one who saved you from the great ape. And I am the one who has come to America to find you, to see if you will love me as I love you."

"She cannot do that," Professor Porter said.

"But why?" Tarzan asked.

The old man hung his head. "It is my fault. Because of my foolishness, we have lost all of our money. I owe ten thousand dollars to a man named Robert Canler. The only way we can keep from losing everything is for Jane to marry Canler. He has come here this week to arrange the wedding."

Tarzan turned to Jane. "Is he the man you wish to marry?" he asked.

"No," she said quietly.

"Jane!" Professor Porter exclaimed. "How can you say that! Mr. Canler has been a great friend of the family! I thought you shared my high opinion of him."

She turned to the professor. "I am sorry, Father," she said, "I have meant to say this to you for a long time. I know you admire him, but I do not. He is a greedy, cruel man who is twice my age. I despise him!"

"Good evening," a stern voice said.

They turned and saw the tall figure of Robert Canler standing in the doorway.

Chapter Twelve

The professor smiled nervously. "Ah, Mr. Canler, how good of you to join us," he said. "May I introduce Tarzan, Tarzan of the Apes."

Canler chuckled. He strode across the room and gripped the ape man's hand.

"Tarzan of the Apes?" he said. "Is this some kind of joke?"

In the blink of an eye, the law of the jungle took over. Tarzan's hand shot forward and seized Canler by the neck, lifting him into the air. The business-man's eyes bulged from their sockets. The ape man shook him, like a cat shakes a mouse.

"Tarzan, stop!" Jane shouted. "You're killing him!"

"You want him to live?" he asked.

"Yes!" she said.

Tarzan dropped Canler on the floor. He glared down into the man's terrified face. "I should kill you now," the ape man growled. "I know what you are trying to do. You are trying to make Jane Porter your wife when you know very well that she does not want you. What kind of man does that to a woman? I will ask you now: Will you go away and never bother Jane Porter again?"

Canler was still trying to catch his breath. He swallowed many times before he could answer. "Yes, I promise," he said at last.

Tarzan grabbed Canler by the collar and pulled him roughly to his feet. "Now, get out," Tarzan of the Apes commanded. "And if you ever bother Jane Porter again, I will skin you alive."

Without bothering to look back, Robert Canler limped from the room, slamming the door behind him. A moment later, they heard his car drive away.

"Look here," Professor Porter said angrily, "what gives you the right to come barging in here and interfere in our affairs this way?"

Tarzan turned and faced the professor. "I know that your daughter does not love this Canler—that is enough for me. It should be enough for you as well."

The professor's shoulders slumped, and his hand went to his forehead. "It should," the professor admitted. "Forgive me, Tarzan. I should know better than to endanger my daughter's happiness. But I owe the man a great deal of money."

"Not for long," Tarzan said. "I found the treasure that was stolen from you. And I have come to make sure that you receive that which is rightfully yours." He drew an envelope from his jacket and handed it to the astonished professor. "Here is a letter from a bank in Paris stating that the treasure was valued at two hundred forty-one thousand dollars. You are a rich man, Professor. You and Jane can do as you like."

Professor Porter read the letter and leaped with joy. "Jane!" he cried. "It is true. We are free. You can marry whomever you wish."

Tarzan turned to Jane. His eyes bored deep into hers. It was as if he were looking into the depths of a jungle pool. "Whom do you wish to marry?" he asked.

Jane bit her lower lip and glanced down. "I don't know," she said. "I am so confused. I knew that I didn't want to marry Canler. But William also has proposed to me. He is a fine man from a fine English family. If William and I married and we moved to England, I would be Lady Greystoke."

"But, Jane," Tarzan said, "tell me

this: When we were in the jungle, you looked at me as if you loved me. Did you love me then? And do you love me now?"

"It's not that simple," she said, taking a deep breath. "Tarzan, listen to me: You are the most magnificent man I have ever seen. To me, you are like something out of a storybook. But it takes more than that to make a happy marriage. We are from different worlds. I don't know if I could survive in the jungle. And you—you would die of boredom if you stayed here. It would kill the part of you that I love most!"

Tarzan nodded sadly. He knew she was right. "But, still," he said, "I want to be near you, to see you and talk to you every day. Don't you want to be near me?"

But before Jane could answer, the front door opened. William Clayton came in from the darkness and shrugged out of his coat. He stopped when he saw Tarzan.

"William!" the professor said. "This is our old friend Tarzan! He has come all the way around the world to return our stolen treasure!"

The Englishman was stunned. "You are Tarzan?" William said. "Why, you are the one who saved my life!" Then, as if he was remembering something, he reached into his coat pocket. "This is incredible!" William said. "I was just checking the mail at the train station when a clerk at the telegraph office told me that a man named Tarzan had arrived and had gone out to the Porter farm. The clerk asked me to bring him this message."

Tarzan opened the envelope. It was a telegram from D'Arnot.

The message read:

CONGRATULATIONS. FINGERPRINTS PROVE YOU
ARE LORD GREYSTOKE.

YOUR FRIEND, D'ARNOT.

Everyone was looking at Tarzan. The room was very quiet.

"What is it?" Jane asked.

Tarzan quietly folded the paper and put it in his pocket. For a moment, he could only stare at the floor. He could not bring himself to look into their expectant faces.

Now Tarzan knew the truth. D'Arnot was right: Tarzan was Johnny Clayton. He was the rightful heir to the Greystoke fortune, not William. Everything his cousin had inherited really belonged to him.

Tarzan knew that if he spoke up, William would be ruined. He would lose his title and his land and his bank accounts. Maybe Jane would not want to marry him. If she knew I was Lord Greystoke, Tarzan thought, she might want to marry me instead.

But as soon as the thought entered his head, he cast it away. He remembered what Jane had said. She was right: They were from different worlds. And he knew, deep in his bones, that William would do everything he could to make her happy and that they could make a good life together.

"What did it say?" William urged.

Tarzan smiled sadly. "It was simply a message from Lieutenant D'Arnot, from Paris. He said that he has completely recovered from his wounds and that he wishes nothing but happiness for all of his friends in America."

William grinned. He looked at Jane with shining eyes. Then William said, "You are a wonderful fellow, Tarzan. It was so good of you to travel all the way to America to return Professor Porter's treasure. Jane and I owe you so much and will always consider you a great friend. I hope you will stay on with us and enjoy the fruits of civilization. By the way, I have often wondered: How did you ever end up in that horrible jungle?"

Tarzan spoke so softly that William could hardly hear. "I was born in the jungle," Tarzan said. "My mother was the great ape, Kala. I never knew anything about my father."

Then he surprised everyone by saying good night and walking out the door, into the Wisconsin night.

Jane followed him down the lane and caught up to him just before he reached the edge of the trees. When he turned to her, Tarzan saw tears in her eyes.

"Tarzan," she said, "where are you going? What will you do now?"

The jungle man stopped and turned to look at her one last time. "I will go back to where I belong," he said simply.

Then, before she could answer, her forest man had slipped away, into the quiet of the night.

About Robin Moore

Robin Moore is a writer and world traveler who enjoys visiting the places that appear in his books. He and his wife spent three weeks camping and traveling through the African grasslands, where they got a close look at many of the animals that appear in the Tarzan story. On one memorable night, two lions made a kill just outside the door of their tent and spent several hours devouring the carcass and growling at the travelers.

Robin still loves to travel. He lives with his family in a stone farmhouse in Springhouse, Pennsylvania.

Be sure to look for Robin Moore's adaptations of *Hercules* and *The Hunchback of Notre Dame,* written especially for young readers.

About
Edgar Rice Burroughs

Edgar Rice Burroughs lived an exciting and productive life. Beginning with his first novel, *The Princess of Mars*, in 1912, he wrote ninety-one books and had many real-life adventures that fueled his fertile imagination.

Born in 1857 to a wealthy family in Chicago, Burroughs served as a member of the United States Cavalry and worked as a miner in Oregon, a cowboy in Idaho, and a policeman in Utah. During World War II, he spent four years in the Pacific, covering the war for U.S. newspapers.

Although he spent his final years confined to a wheelchair, Burroughs's imagination continued to run wild: When he died in 1950, he left fifteen unpublished manuscripts.

He lived to see the story of Tarzan spread around the globe. His books were translated into fifty-six languages and sold in the millions, making him one of the world's most popular writers.